Paulette Bogan

VIRGIL & OWEN

BLOOMSBURY
NEW YORK   LONDON   NEW DELHI   SYDNEY

First published in the United States of America in January 2015
by Bloomsbury Children's Books
www.bloomsbury.com

Bloomsbury is a registered trademark of Bloomsbury Publishing Plc

For information about permission to reproduce selections from this book, write to
Permissions, Bloomsbury Children's Books, 1385 Broadway, New York, New York 10018
Bloomsbury books may be purchased for business or promotional use. For information on bulk purchases
please contact Macmillan Corporate and Premium Sales Department at specialmarkets@macmillan.com

Library of Congress Cataloging-in-Publication Data
Bogan, Paulette, author, illustrator.
Virgil & Owen / by Paulette Bogan.
pages   cm
Summary: Virgil the penguin finds a polar bear and tries to claim it as his own, but the polar bear wants to
splash with the terns, slide with the seals, twirl with all the penguins, and be called by his name—Owen.
ISBN 978-1-61963-372-8 (hardcover)
ISBN 978-1-61963-514-2 (e-book) • ISBN 978-1-61963-513-5 (e-PDF)
[1. Friendship—Fiction. 2. Penguins—Fiction. 3. Polar bear—Fiction.
4. Bears—Fiction.] I. Title. II. Title: Virgil and Owen.
PZ7.B6357835Vir 2015   [E]—dc23   2014009097

Art created with Sakura Micron pens (waterproof) and Winsor Newton Water Colour,
on Arches cold press watercolor paper
Typeset in Bodoni Egyptian
Book design by Amanda Bartlett

Printed in China by Leo Paper Products, Heshan, Guangdong
1 3 5 7 9 10 8 6 4 2

Love and thanks to

My friends, Luke and Noah Eisman

My girls, Soph, Rach, and Lulu

My other brain, Simone Kaplan

"I found a polar bear, Mom," said Virgil,

"and I'm keeping him."

"You are my polar bear," said Virgil.

"Come with me."

The polar bear splished and splashed
with the terns. Everyone laughed.

Virgil did not laugh.

"You are my polar bear," said Virgil.

"Come with me."

The polar bear slipped and slid with
the seals. Everyone had fun.

Virgil did not have fun.

"You are *my* polar bear," said Virgil.

"Come with *me*."

The polar bear twirled and whirled with
the penguins. Everyone had a wonderful time.
Virgil did not have a wonderful time.

"Stop it," said Virgil. "You are **my** polar bear! Come with **me**!"

"No," said the polar bear, "and my
name is Owen."

Virgil stomped away.

He kicked the snow.

He jumped up and down.

"Come play with us," said Owen.

"Really?" said Virgil.

Everyone dipped and dived, splashed
and swam, and played together.

Until . . .

"Listen to me, Owen," said Virgil.

"You are *not* my polar bear . . ."

"You are my friend."

Everyone cheered, "We are all friends!"